To Abe, Leo, and Della, with love
M. B.

For my mom and dad, who bought me
my first bike with pop-bottle deposits
N. Z. J.

Text copyright © 2016 by Maribeth Boelts
Illustrations copyright © 2016 by Noah Z. Jones

First edition 2016

Library of Congress Catalog Card Number 2015909440
ISBN 978-0-7636-6649-1

16 17 18 19 20 21 APS 10 9 8 7 6 5 4 3 2 1

Printed in Humen, Dongguan, China

MIX
Paper from
responsible sources
FSC® C101537

This book was typeset in Frutiger.
The illustrations were done in watercolor, pencil, and ink and assembled digitally.

Candlewick Press
99 Dover Street
Somerville, Massachusetts 02144

visit us at www.candlewick.com

A BIKE LIKE SERGIO'S

Maribeth Boelts

illustrated by Noah Z. Jones

CANDLEWICK PRESS

A BIKE LIKE SERGIO'S

Maribeth Boelts

illustrated by Noah Z. Jones

CANDLEWICK PRESS

Every kid has a bike but me.

Sergio rides his new one while I run alongside, out of breath.

"Ask your parents again," Sergio says. "Your birthday's coming."

Sergio forgets there's a difference between his birthday and mine.

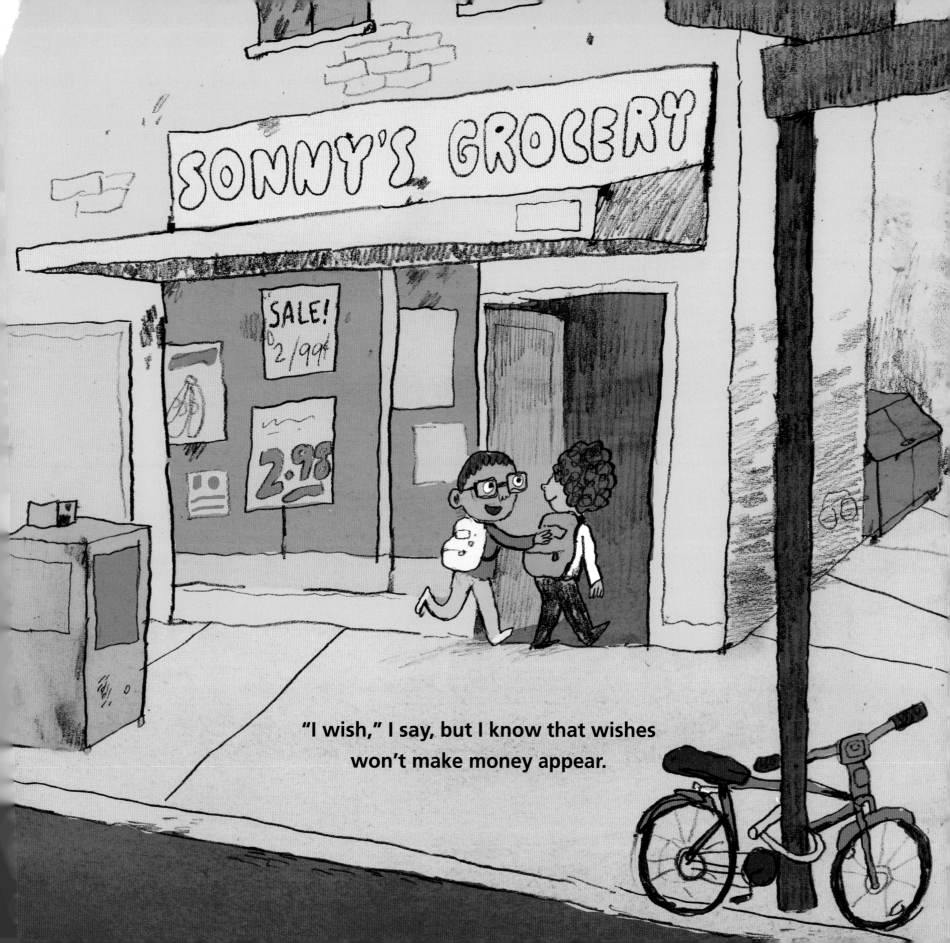

"I wish," I say, but I know that wishes
won't make money appear.

At Sonny's Grocery, Sergio buys a pack of football cards.

I stand in line, mad, with the bread my mom wants, waiting behind the lady in the blue coat who we see all the time.

She steps up to pay and gathers her bags. In the shuffle, her purse tips.

A dollar floats to the floor. No one sees.

I scoop up the money fast.

She's out the door, but I don't chase her—it's just a dollar.

At home, Mom's feeding the baby. The twins pull pans from the cupboard.

"My Ruben," she says. "Was it a good day?"

I nod and act busy. That dollar in my pocket stays a secret.

Later, when I'm alone in my room, I fish out the crumpled bill—and stare.

It is not one dollar or five or ten.

It is *one hundred dollars.*

My hands are shaking.

That money is enough for a bike like Sergio's. Then I won't have to run; I'll be *riding*.

Dad gets home from work late and tucks in my little brothers. When he gets to me, I squeeze my eyes shut and stay still as a stone.

In the morning, the hundred-dollar bill is
safe in my backpack.

When I get to school, Mr. Grady says we will be learning about money in math. He sets up a store with fake bills and coins and pictures of things we can buy. I joke around and blow all my play money on a camera right away.

Me on my bike is all I can think about.

We stop at the bike shop after school.

Inside, I walk the rows and find one like Sergio's,
but silver.

"Man, you look good on it," Sergio says, and it's true.

But I know if I ride home on a bike like that, I'll have to tell my parents where I got the money.

"I'll talk to them tonight," I say, and Sergio high-fives me.

SALE

At home, Mom is making a grocery list for Saturday. She walks her fingers through the cash in her wallet. Then she crosses things off.

"Maybe next week," she says. She looks up at me and smiles.

Me, with the hundred in my backpack. Her, crossing things off.

Then she hands me a five-dollar bill. "On your way home tomorrow, could you pick up orange juice at Sonny's?"

When she mentions Sonny's, I feel the sweat.

What if the lady in the blue coat is there?

I take my stuff to my room, dump my papers out of my backpack, and that's when I see it:

The zipper that was closed is open, just enough.

And the money that was there is gone.

Heading out the door, I mumble to Mom,
"I'll be right back."

Rain is falling as I retrace
my steps from school
to bike shop to home.

Leaves and money
look the same.

Rain and tears feel the same.

It's nowhere.

I walk hunched and draggy to school the next day,
while Sergio rides circles.

"My brother built a ramp in the alley, and I went
airborne!" he says. "If you get that bike, you can use it."

I don't tell Sergio that I won't be getting any bike at all.

The day stretches out. "How many nickels in a dollar?"
Mr. Grady asks. "How many quarters in a five-dollar bill?"

When the bell rings, I pack my backpack with
homework and notes and tell Sergio to ride home
without me.

With everyone crowding in a hurry, I spot something.
The smallest zipper inside—still closed.

This was the pocket, not the other. I slide it open, and I am rich again.

To get that bike, I have to tell.

I race to Sonny's as fast as riding, and rush to the back of the store for the juice.

Someone bumps me, apologizes in a soft voice—I turn.

My feet are frozen, watching as the lady in the blue coat makes her way to the counter with her eggs.

She reaches into her purse.

And like a hot blast, I remember how it was for me when that money that was hers—then mine—was gone.

I leave the juice behind. And this time, I follow her.

She walks down one street, then another.
And past the bike shop.

My mouth is dry.

"Excuse me," I say.

She turns and we are face-to-face.

I breathe fast, and the words bust loose like they've been waiting.

The lady says yes: she lost a hundred dollars, and has been looking since.

She tips her head. "Why?"

I uncurl my fist. "I found it," I say, holding it out to her still folded.

Her face changes from surprised . . . to joyful . . . to soft.

She takes my hand in both of hers like a sandwich and asks my name.

"Thank you, Ruben," she says. "You have blessed me."

I am happy and mixed up, full and empty, with what's right and what's gone.

At home, everyone is waiting, and the lost and found story is mine to tell.

"What you did wasn't easy," my dad says, setting his hand on my shoulder, "but it was right."

My mom pulls me close.

"We're so proud," she says.

And in that warm house, with my family all
around and my birthday almost here . . .
I am proud, too.